UNLEASH YOUR CHAMPION: RISE AND SHINE

TUSHAR RAJ

Made with ♥ on the Notion Press Platform
www.notionpress.com

This book is dedicated to all the dreamers, doers, and go-getters out there who never give up on their aspirations, no matter what life throws their way. Your relentless determination to be the best version of yourselves inspires us all.

To those who have faced setbacks, obstacles, and heartbreak, yet still rise above it all, this book is for you. You have shown us that the human spirit is unbreakable and that with the right mindset and tools, anyone can unleash their inner champion.

To the people who believe in themselves, and never let anyone or anything dim their light, we salute you. Keep shining, keep striving, and never stop dreaming.

With gratitude and admiration,

Tushar Raj

Contents

Foreword

Welcome to "Unleash Your Champion: Rise and Shine," a guide to harnessing the power within and unlocking your full potential. The journey to self-discovery and personal growth is not always easy, but it is always worth it. This book will provide you with the tools and inspiration you need to tap into your inner champion and achieve your goals.

We all have a champion within us, waiting to be unleashed. This champion is the source of our strength, our courage, and our determination. It is the voice that drives us to push beyond our limits and strive for greatness. However, life can be challenging, and it can be difficult to tap into our inner champion when we are faced with obstacles and setbacks. That's why this book was created - to help you find your inner champion and unleash it so that you can reach your full potential.

In these pages, you will learn about the power of positive thinking, the importance of self-belief, and how to overcome fear and adversity. You will discover strategies for setting and achieving your goals, and for living a life of purpose and fulfillment. You will also find inspiration from individuals who have overcome great obstacles to achieve their dreams, and who have learned to harness the power of their inner champion to achieve success and happiness.

So whether you are looking to boost your confidence, improve your relationships, or achieve your dreams, "Unleash Your Champion: Rise and Shine" has something to offer. With the guidance and inspiration contained within these pages, you will be able to unleash your inner champion and rise to the top. So, let's get started on this journey together.

Preface

Welcome to "Unleash Your Champion: Rise and Shine," a guide designed to help you awaken the champion within. This book was created to empower you to take control of your life and reach your full potential. Whether you're looking to improve in a particular area, overcome challenges, or simply live a more fulfilling life, this book is here to help.

In these pages, you'll discover a wealth of knowledge, insights, and practical strategies for unlocking your inner champion. From mastering your mindset and developing a growth-oriented perspective, to setting goals and creating a plan for success, this book covers all the essential elements for achieving your dreams.

The journey to unlocking your inner champion can be a challenging one, but it's also an incredibly rewarding one. By reading this book, you'll gain the tools, knowledge, and confidence to take the first step and begin your journey to greatness.

So, let's get started! This is your moment to

rise and shine, and unleash the champion within. The time to make a positive change in your life is now. Let's do this!

Acknowledgements

The journey of writing this book was long and challenging, but it wouldn't have been possible without the support and encouragement of so many people.

Firstly, I want to express my gratitude to my family, who believed in me even when I didn't believe in myself. Your love and support provided me with the foundation to chase my dreams and live a fulfilling life.

I am also thankful for the wonderful team at OpenAI, who provided me with the tools and resources necessary to write this book. I would like to give a special shoutout to the amazing editors and proofreaders who helped make this book a reality.

I want to acknowledge all of my readers, who have provided me with the motivation to keep writing and sharing my message of hope and positivity. Your feedback and support have been invaluable, and I am grateful for every message and email I receive from each of you.

Lastly, I would like to thank the universe for its endless possibilities and for guiding me on this amazing journey. I am filled with gratitude for the opportunities and experiences that have shaped my life and allowed me to grow as a person.

Thank you all for your unwavering support and encouragement."

Prologue

Do you ever feel like you are just going through the motions of life? Do you have dreams and aspirations that seem just out of reach? Do you feel like there is more to life but you just don't know how to unlock it?

It is time to awaken the champion within you. The person you were meant to be. The person who is confident, successful, and fulfilled. The person who knows what they want and goes after it with passion and purpose.

This book is your guide to unlocking your full potential. Within these pages, you will find the tools, techniques, and inspiration you need to rise and shine. To take control of your life and achieve your dreams. To become the champion you were born to be.

You have the power within you to create the life you desire. The first step is to believe in yourself. The second step is to take action. And the third step is to never give up.

So, are you ready to unleash your inner

champion? It's time to rise and shine!

ONE

Discovering Your Purpose

Have you ever felt lost or unfulfilled in life? Like there has to be something more, but you just don't know what it is? If so, you're not alone. Many people struggle with finding their purpose and feeling fulfilled in life.

Discovering your purpose is a crucial step in unleashing your inner champion and creating a life filled with passion and meaning. It's the foundation upon which you can build a successful and fulfilling life.

So, how do you discover your purpose? Start by taking the time to reflect on what you enjoy doing, what makes you feel fulfilled, and what you're good at. Think about your values, beliefs, and what you want to contribute to the world. Consider your past experiences and what you've learned from them.

Once you have a better understanding of what is important to you and what you enjoy, start exploring potential career paths and interests that align with your values and passions. Take small steps towards your goals, try new things, and be open to new opportunities.

Remember, discovering your purpose is a journey, not a destination. So don't be discouraged if it takes some time.

Another way to discover your purpose is to seek guidance from those around you. Talk to friends, family, and mentors who know you well and can provide you with insights and support. You can also try journaling, meditating, or participating in activities that bring you a sense of peace and clarity.

Finding your purpose can be a challenging but rewarding journey. It's an opportunity to discover what makes you truly happy and fulfilled. And when you find your purpose, you'll be one step closer to unlocking your inner champion and creating the life you desire.

So, take the first step today. Start exploring what is important to you and what brings you joy. And never stop searching for your purpose. The journey may be difficult, but the reward is a life filled with meaning and fulfillment.

Exercise

Exercise: Discovering Your Purpose

(DO IT YOURSELF)

1. Reflect on your values, beliefs, and what is important to you. Write a list of these things and consider how they influence your life.

2. Think about your past experiences, what you've learned from them, and what you enjoy doing. Write a list of these things and reflect on how they might play a role in discovering your purpose.

3. Identify your strengths and areas for improvement. Write a list of your skills and areas where you excel, as well as areas where you would like to improve.

4. Consider your passions and interests. Write a list of things you are passionate about and activities that bring you joy.

5. Brainstorm potential career paths and interests that align with your values, passions, and strengths. Write a list of these ideas and think about how you might pursue them.

6. Talk to people you trust, such as friends, family, or mentors, and seek their insights and support. Ask them what they think you are good at and what they think your

purpose in life might be.

7. Journal or meditate on your thoughts and feelings as you explore what is important to you and what brings you joy. This can help you gain a deeper understanding of your purpose.

8. Take small steps towards your goals, try new things, and be open to new opportunities. The journey to discovering your purpose may take time, but each step will bring you closer to your goal.

9. Be patient and persistent. Discovering your purpose is a journey, not a destination. Keep exploring what is important to you and what brings you joy.

10. Celebrate your progress and be proud of yourself for taking the first step towards discovering your purpose. This is an important step in unleashing your inner champion and creating the life you desire.

TWO

OVERCOMING SELF-DOUBT

Self-doubt can be a major roadblock on the path to success. It can hold us back from pursuing our dreams, trying new things, and stepping out of our comfort zones. But the good news is, self-doubt is something that can be overcome.

** Here are some tips to help you conquer self-doubt and unleash your inner champion:*

1. ***Recognize your self-doubt:*** The first step in overcoming self-doubt is to acknowledge its presence. Recognize when you're feeling uncertain or insecure and understand that these feelings are normal.
2. ***Challenge your negative thoughts:*** When you catch yourself having negative thoughts, ask yourself if they are truly accurate. Often, our self-doubt is based on false beliefs or past experiences that don't reflect our current reality.
3. ***Surround yourself with positivity:*** Surround yourself with positive people who believe in you and encourage you.

Their support can hclp counteract the negative thoughts that feed your self-doubt.

4. ***Celebrate your successes:*** Focus on your accomplishments, no matter how small they may be. Celebrate your successes and remind yourself of your abilities and strengths.

5. ***Embrace fear***: Fear can often be a driving force behind self-doubt. Embrace your fear and use it as fuel to push yourself forward. Recognize that fear is just a feeling and can be overcome.

By following these steps, you can overcome self-doubt and become the confident, self-assured person you were meant to be. Remember, everyone, experiences self-doubt at times. The key is to recognize it and take action to overcome it. You have the power within you to conquer self-doubt and unleash your inner champion.

Exercise

This exercise is designed to help you identify and challenge your self-doubt, and develop more confidence in yourself.

1. Write down a list of your self-doubt thoughts: Write down all the negative thoughts that are holding you back. Include anything from "I'm not good enough" to "I'll never be able to do that."

2. Challenge your negative thoughts: For each thought, ask yourself if it's truly accurate. Write down evidence that proves the opposite, such as previous experiences where you succeeded or compliments you've received from others.

3. Replace negative thoughts with positive affirmations: Write down positive affirmations to counteract your negative thoughts. For example, if your negative thought is "I'll never be able to do that," your positive affirmation could be "I am capable and competent, and I will succeed." Repeat your affirmations to yourself every day.

4. Surround yourself with positivity: Spend time with people who believe in you and encourage you. Seek out positive experiences and engage in activities that make you feel good about yourself.

5. Celebrate your successes: Focus on your accomplishments, no matter how small they may be. Celebrate your successes and remind yourself of your abilities and strengths.

Repeat this exercise regularly to help you overcome self-doubt and develop greater confidence in yourself. Remember, self-doubt is a normal feeling, but it doesn't have to hold you back. You have the power to overcome it and unleash your inner champion.

THREE

BUILDING CONFIDENCE

Confidence is the key to unlocking your full potential and becoming the champion you were meant to be. When you have confidence, you believe in yourself and your abilities. You are not afraid to take risks and chase your dreams. You are comfortable in your own skin and are not held back by self-doubt or insecurity.

**** Building confidence is a journey, not a destination. It takes time and effort to develop, but the reward is worth it. Here are some practical tips to help you build your confidence:***

1. ***Practice self-care.*** Taking care of yourself physically and mentally is essential for building confidence. Exercise regularly, eat well, and get enough sleep. Also, practice mindfulness and positive self-talk.

2. ***Set achievable goals.*** Accomplishing small tasks can give you a boost of confidence. Set goals that are achievable

and focus on progress, not perfection. Celebrate your successes, no matter how small they may be.

3. ***Surround yourself with positive people.*** Surrounding yourself with positive and supportive people can have a significant impact on your confidence. Seek relationships with people who believe in you and your abilities.

4. ***Embrace your uniqueness.*** Confidence comes from accepting and embracing who you are. Stop comparing yourself to others and focus on your strengths and abilities.

5. ***Face your fears.*** Confidence is built by taking action, even in the face of fear. Identify the things that hold you back and take small steps to overcome them. Remember, confidence is developed through repeated experiences of success.

Remember, building confidence is a journey and not a destination. It takes time and effort, but the reward is worth it. When you have confidence, you have the power to achieve your dreams and become the champion you were meant to be.

So, go ahead and take the first step. Believe in yourself, take action, and never give up. The confidence you need to succeed is within you.

Exercise

Exercise: Building Confidence

One effective way to build confidence is through journaling. This exercise will help you reflect on your strengths and accomplishments and give you a boost of confidence.

Instructions:

1. Get a journal or a piece of paper and a pen.

2. Write down five things you are proud of that you have accomplished in the past. It could be anything from landing your first job to overcoming a personal challenge.

3. Write down five things you are good at. These can be skills, talents, or qualities that you possess.

4. Write down five things you have learned from your past experiences and how they have made you stronger.

5. Write down five things you would like to accomplish in the future and why they are important to you.

Once you have completed the exercise, take some time to reflect on your answers. Read over your list of accomplishments, strengths, and future goals. Remind yourself of how far

you have come and what you are capable of. This exercise is a powerful tool for building confidence and will give you a boost of self-esteem.

So, take the time to do this exercise and invest in building your confidence. Remember, when you have confidence, you have the power to achieve your dreams and become the champion you were meant to be.

FOUR

SETTING AND ACHIEVING GOALS

Welcome to Chapter 4 of Unleash Your Champion: Rise and Shine! In this chapter, we will be discussing the importance of setting and achieving goals and how they can help you unlock your full potential.

Goals give us direction and purpose. They give us something to work towards and help us focus our energy and efforts. Setting and achieving goals can help you feel more in control of your life and give you a sense of accomplishment and satisfaction.

So, how do we set and achieve our goals? The first step is to define what you want. Take some time to think about what is truly important to you. What do you want to achieve in your personal life? What do you want to achieve in your professional life? What kind of person do you want to be?

Once you have a clear idea of what you want, it's time to create specific and measurable goals. Instead of saying, "I want to be successful," try saying, "I want to increase my income by 25% within the next year." This is a specific and measurable goal that you can work towards.

Next, create an action plan. What steps will you need to take to achieve your goal? Break down your goal into smaller, manageable steps and create a timeline for when you want to complete each step.

Finally, it's time to take action. Start working on your action plan and focus on making progress every day. Celebrate your successes, no matter how small they may be, and keep your focus on your ultimate goal.

Remember, the key to achieving your goals is to stay focused, take consistent action, and never give up.

In conclusion, setting and achieving goals is a powerful tool to help you unleash your inner champion and create the life you desire. Start defining what you want, creating specific and measurable goals, and taking action today!

Exercise

Exercise: Setting and Achieving Goals

This exercise is designed to help you set and achieve your goals. Follow these steps to get started:

1. Write down your goals: Take some time to think about what you want to achieve. Write down your personal and professional goals and be as specific and measurable as possible.

2. Prioritize your goals: Once you have a list of your goals, prioritize them. Which goals are most important to you and why?

3. Create an action plan: For each goal, break it down into smaller, manageable steps and create a timeline for when you want to complete each step.

4. Take action: Start working on your action plan and focus on making progress every day.

5. Track your progress: Keep track of your progress towards each goal. Celebrate your successes and stay focused on your ultimate goal.

6. Review and adjust: Regularly review your goals and action plans. Are you making progress? Do you need to make any adjustments to your plan?

7. Stay motivated: Stay motivated by reminding yourself why each goal is important to you and how achieving it will help you unleash your inner champion.

By following these steps, you will be well on your way to setting and achieving your goals. Remember, the key is to stay focused, take consistent action, and never give up. Good luck!

FIVE

DEVELOPING A GROWTH MINDSET

Have you ever heard the saying, "Success is 10% inspiration and 90% perspiration"? Well, this statement couldn't be truer when it comes to developing a growth mindset. A growth mindset is a belief that you can grow and improve through effort and learning. It's the opposite of a fixed mindset, which is the belief that your abilities are set and cannot be changed.

So, how do you develop a growth mindset? It all starts with a change in your thinking. Instead of focusing on what you can't do, focus on what you can do. Look for opportunities to learn and grow, rather than reasons why you can't. Embrace challenges and embrace failure as a learning opportunity, not a reason to give up.

Here are some tips for developing a growth mindset:

1. ***Practice self-reflection:*** Take time to reflect on your thoughts, beliefs, and attitudes. Be honest with yourself about areas where you have a fixed mindset and make a conscious effort to shift your thinking.

2. ***Embrace challenges:*** Don't shy away from challenges. Embrace them as opportunities to grow and learn. Look at challenges as a means to improve, rather than as a barrier to success.

3. ***Celebrate progress:*** Celebrate your progress, no matter how small. Recognize that progress, not perfection, is what matters.

4. ***Surround yourself with growth-minded individuals:*** Surround yourself with individuals who have a growth mindset. They will inspire and motivate you to be the best version of yourself.

5. ***Learn from failure:*** Instead of dwelling on failure, view it as an opportunity to learn and grow. Ask yourself, "What can I learn from this experience?"

Developing a growth mindset takes time and effort, but the benefits are worth it. With a growth mindset, you will be able to tackle any challenge and achieve your goals. You will be able to unlock your full potential and become the champion you were meant to be. So, embrace the growth mindset and watch your life transform!

Exercise

Exercise: Developing a Growth Mindset

One of the best ways to develop a growth mindset is to practice it daily. This exercise will help you to focus your thoughts and beliefs on growth and improvement, and to cultivate a positive, growth-oriented mindset.

1. Write down a fixed mindset believe that you have. For example, "I'm not good at public speaking" or "I can never be good at math."

2. Re-frame this belief into a growth mindset statement. For example, "I may not be good at public speaking now, but with practice and effort, I can improve" or "I may struggle with math, but I can learn and grow in this area with hard work and determination."

3. Repeat this process for several other fixed mindset beliefs that you have.

4. Write down a goal that you have, and then write down the steps you need to take to achieve that goal.

5. Reflect on your goal and the steps you need to take to achieve it. Focus on the growth and learning opportunities that these steps offer, rather than on any obstacles or challenges.

6. Repeat this process daily, or as often as needed, to cultivate a growth mindset.

Remember, developing a growth mindset takes time and effort, but the benefits are worth it. With a growth mindset, you will be able to tackle any challenge and achieve your goals. So, be patient, be persistent, and watch your life transform!

SIX

EMBRACING FAILURE AND LEARNING FROM MISTAKES

"Success is not final, failure is not fatal: it is the courage to continue those counts." - Winston Churchill

Embracing failure and learning from mistakes is a crucial step in the journey to unleashing your inner champion. Despite what society may tell us, failure is not a bad thing. It's actually an opportunity to grow and learn. Every failure is a chance to get up, dust yourself off, and try again. And every time you try again, you become stronger and more resilient.

But, why do we fear failure so much? Often, it's because we've been taught to believe that failure is a reflection of our abilities. We're taught that failure is a sign of weakness and that it should be avoided at all costs. This couldn't be further from the truth. In reality, failure is a natural part of life and a necessary step toward success.

The key to embracing failure is to reframe it. Instead of seeing it as a negative, see it as an opportunity to learn and grow. Every failure is a lesson, and every lesson is a stepping stone toward success.

So, how can you learn from your mistakes? Start by analyzing what went wrong. Ask yourself questions like: "What could I have done differently?" "What did I learn from this experience?" "What can I do to prevent this from happening again?" These questions will help you identify areas for improvement and give you the knowledge you need to succeed in the future.

It's also important to forgive yourself and move on. Holding onto negative feelings about your failures will only hold you back. Instead, focus on the lessons you've learned and use them to make progress.

In conclusion, embracing failure and learning from mistakes is a critical part of the journey to unleashing your inner champion. Remember, every failure is an opportunity to grow and learn. So, embrace it, learn from it, and never give up.

Exercise

Exercise: Embracing Failure and Learning from Mistakes

1. Write down a recent failure: Take a moment to reflect on a recent failure or mistake. Write down what happened, how it made you feel, and what you learned from the experience.

2. Reframe the failure: Reframe your failure as an opportunity to learn and grow. Write down the positive aspects of the experience and what you can do differently next time.

3. Analyze the failure: Analyze what went wrong and what you could have done differently. Ask yourself questions like: "What could I have done differently?" "What did I learn from this experience?" "What can I do to prevent this from happening again?"

4. Forgive yourself: Forgive yourself for your failure and move on. Write down what you can do to let go of any negative feelings and focus on the lessons you've learned.

5. Implement the lessons: Use the lessons you've learned from your failure to make progress. Write down specific steps you can take to ensure success in the future.

Repeat this exercise whenever you experience a failure. Over time, you'll develop a growth mindset and become more resilient to failure. Embracing failure and learning from mistakes will become a natural part of your journey to unleashing your inner champion.

SEVEN

Cultivating a Positive Mindset

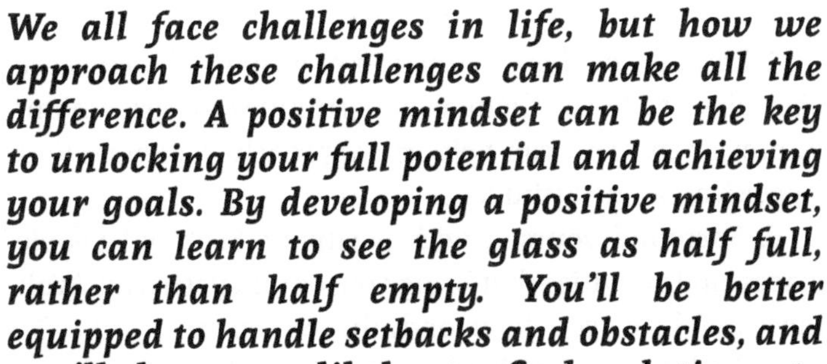

We all face challenges in life, but how we approach these challenges can make all the difference. A positive mindset can be the key to unlocking your full potential and achieving your goals. By developing a positive mindset, you can learn to see the glass as half full, rather than half empty. You'll be better equipped to handle setbacks and obstacles, and you'll be more likely to find solutions to problems.

So, how do you cultivate a positive mindset? Here are some tips to get started:

1. Practice gratitude: Take time each day to reflect on the things you're thankful for. This can help you focus on the positive aspects of your life and reduce feelings of negativity and stress.

2. Surround yourself with positivity: Seek out people, places, and activities that bring you joy and positivity. Avoid those that bring you down or drain your energy.

3. Reframe negative thoughts: When negative thoughts arise, try to reframe them in a more positive light. For example, instead of thinking, "I can never do anything right," try thinking, "I've learned from my mistakes and I'll do better next time."

4. Focus on the present moment: It's easy to get caught up in worries about the future or regrets about the past, but both of these things are outside of our control. By focusing on the present moment, you can appreciate what you have right now and cultivate a positive mindset.

5. Embrace challenges: Instead of viewing challenges as obstacles, try to see them as opportunities for growth and improvement. This can help you approach challenges with a positive, can-do attitude.

6. Surround yourself with positivity: Seek out people, places, and activities that bring you joy and positivity. Avoid those that bring you down or drain your energy.

7. Find the good in difficult situations: When faced with a difficult situation, try to find the silver lining. This can help you maintain a positive outlook and find the opportunities hidden within challenges.

By cultivating a positive mindset, you'll be better equipped to handle life's ups and downs

and achieve your goals. Remember, a positive mindset is a choice – so choose it every day!

Exercise

Exercise: Cultivating a Positive Mindset

One of the most effective ways to cultivate a positive mindset is to practice positive self-talk. This means speaking to yourself in a supportive and encouraging manner, rather than criticizing or belittling yourself. This exercise will help you get started.

1. Write down negative self-talk: Spend some time reflecting on the things you often say to yourself. Write down any negative or critical thoughts that come to mind.

2. Reframe your negative self-talk: For each negative thought, try to reframe it in a more positive light. For example, instead of thinking "I'm so lazy," try thinking, "I'm taking the time I need to recharge and renew my energy."

3. Practice positive self-talk: Choose one or two of the reframed thoughts from step 2 and make a conscious effort to repeat them to yourself throughout the day. You can also write them down and post them in a place where you will see them often.

4. Track your progress: Keep a journal to track your progress with this exercise. Each day, write down any negative self-talk that comes up and try to reframe it in a positive light.

5. Celebrate your progress: When you notice that your self-talk has become more positive, take a moment to celebrate your progress. You're taking a big step toward cultivating a positive mindset.

By making a conscious effort to reframe your negative self-talk, you can train your brain to focus on the positive aspects of your life. This exercise is just one of many that you can use to cultivate a positive mindset, so keep exploring and experimenting with new techniques that work for you!

EIGHT

Building Strong Relationships

The foundation of every successful personal or professional life is a strong network of relationships. Whether it is with friends, family, colleagues, or partners, forming and maintaining healthy relationships can bring joy, support, and growth into our lives. In this chapter, we will explore some of the key principles and practices of building strong relationships.

1. ***Communication:*** Communication is the foundation of every relationship. It is essential to actively listen to each other, express our thoughts and feelings clearly, and be

open to feedback. Try to avoid misunderstandings by asking for clarification and repeating important information. It is also important to find common ground and respect each other's opinions and perspectives, even if you don't agree.

2. ***Trust:*** Trust is the glue that holds relationships together. Building trust takes time, but it can be accelerated by being honest, reliable, and keeping your promises. If trust is broken, it can be difficult to regain, so it's important to handle conflicts with care and address them openly and respectfully.

3. ***Empathy:*** Empathy is the ability to understand and share the feelings of others. Showing empathy allows you to connect with others on a deeper level and understand their motivations and perspectives. Practice putting yourself in others' shoes and asking questions to understand their experiences.

4. ***Support:*** Strong relationships are built on mutual support. Offer help and support when your friends, family, or colleagues need it and don't be afraid to ask for help when you need it. Supporting each other through tough times can strengthen your relationship and build a deep bond.

5. ***Gratitude:*** Expressing gratitude is a powerful tool for building strong relationships. Take time to acknowledge the contributions and efforts of others, and express appreciation for their support and friendship. Saying thank you goes a long way in making someone feel valued and appreciated.

6. ***Quality Time:*** Spending quality time with your loved ones, friends, and colleagues is an essential aspect of building strong relationships. This can be done through shared activities, conversation, or simply being present and

attentive.

Conclusion: Building strong relationships take time and effort, but it is a rewarding and fulfilling process. By communicating openly, building trust, showing empathy, offering support, expressing gratitude, and spending quality time together, you can create deep and meaningful connections that will enrich your life. Remember, every relationship is unique, and what works for one may not work for another, so it's important to be flexible and adaptable. Happy relationship building!

Exercise

Exercise: Building Strong Relationships

In this exercise, we will focus on improving communication and strengthening our relationships.

Step 1: Reflect on your current relationships. Take a moment to think about the relationships in your life and consider the following questions:

* How well do you communicate with each person in your life?

* Do you feel heard and understood?

* Are there any areas where you can improve your communication?

Step 2: Identify areas for improvement. Make a list of any communication challenges you face in your relationships. This may include avoiding difficult conversations, not expressing your feelings, or assuming you know what someone else is thinking or feeling.

Step 3: Practice active listening. When communicating with someone, make an effort to truly listen to what they have to say. Avoid interrupting, ask questions to clarify, and show that you are engaged in the conversation.

Step 4: Be open and honest. Share your thoughts and feelings with the people in your life. Be authentic and avoid hiding your true self. Remember, vulnerability can build trust and strengthen relationships.

Step 5: Show appreciation and gratitude. Acknowledge and appreciate the people in your life. Express gratitude for their support and let them know that you value them.

By practicing these steps, you can improve your communication and build stronger relationships. Remember, relationships take effort and commitment, but the rewards of having strong connections with others are immeasurable.

NINE

Taking Action and Staying Motivated

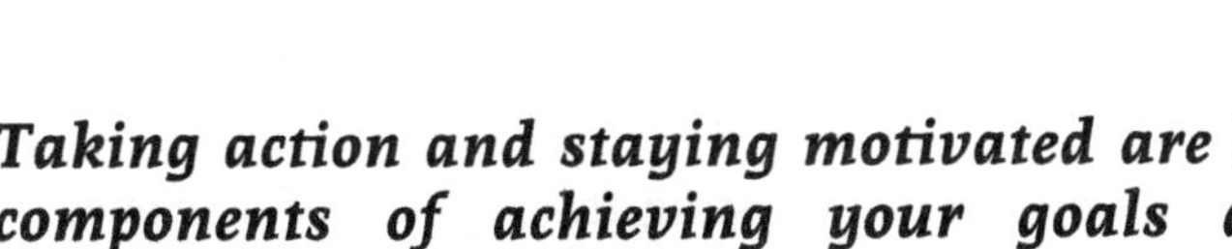

Taking action and staying motivated are key components of achieving your goals and unlocking your full potential. In this chapter, we will explore practical strategies for taking action toward your goals and maintaining motivation along the way.

1. ***Identify your goals:*** The first step in taking action is to identify what you want to achieve. Write down your personal and professional goals, both short-term and long-term. Ensure that your goals are specific, measurable, achievable, relevant, and time-bound (SMART). This will help you focus your efforts and measure your progress.
2. ***Break down your goals into smaller tasks:*** Breaking down your goals into smaller, manageable tasks can help

make them feel more achievable. This can help you stay motivated and see progress along the way.

3. ***Create a plan of action:*** Having a clear plan of action is essential for taking action. Write down the tasks and deadlines for each goal. Be sure to include specific dates and times for each task. This will help you stay organized and on track.

4. ***Take action:*** The most important step in taking action is to start. Focus on taking small, consistent steps toward your goal. Celebrate each accomplishment and continue to take action until you reach your goal.

5. ***Celebrate progress:*** It's important to acknowledge and celebrate your progress along the way. Taking time to recognize your efforts will help keep you motivated and focused on your goal.

6. ***Stay motivated:*** Staying motivated can be a challenge, but there are strategies that can help. Set up a system of reminders and accountability to help keep yourself motivated. This may include setting aside time each day to work on your goals, enlisting the support of a friend, or finding a mentor or coach.

By taking action and staying motivated, you will be able to achieve your goals and unleash your inner champion. Remember, success requires effort and determination, but the rewards of reaching your goals are worth it!

Exercise

Exercise: Taking Action and Staying Motivated

In this exercise, we will focus on taking action toward your goals and maintaining motivation.

Step 1: Identify your goals. Make a list of your personal and professional goals, both short-term and long-term. Ensure that your goals are specific, measurable, achievable, relevant, and time-bound (SMART).

Step 2: Break down your goals into smaller, achievable tasks. Divide each goal into smaller, manageable steps. This will help you see progress and make the goal feel more achievable.

Step 3: Create a plan of action. Write down the tasks and deadlines for each goal. Be sure to include specific dates and times for each task.

Step 4: Take action. Start working on your plan by completing the first task. Focus on taking small, consistent steps toward your goal.

Step 5: Celebrate your progress. As you complete each task, take time to celebrate your progress and acknowledge your efforts. This will help keep you motivated and focused.

Step 6: Stay motivated. Set up a system of reminders and accountability to help keep yourself motivated. This may include setting aside time each day to work on your goals, enlisting the support of a friend, or finding a mentor or coach.

By taking action and staying motivated, you will be able to achieve your goals and unleash your inner champion. Remember, success requires effort and determination, but the rewards of reaching your goals are worth it!

TEN

Living a Fulfilled Life

Congratulations, you've made it to the final chapter! In this chapter, we will focus on how to live a fulfilled life, one that is meaningful, joyful, and rich in experiences. A life that you will look back on with pride and satisfaction. So, let's get started!

1. ***Reflect on what makes you happy:*** The first step in living a fulfilling life is to understand what brings you happiness and joy. Take some time to reflect on the activities and experiences that make you feel fulfilled. This could be spending time with loved ones, traveling, volunteering, or pursuing a hobby. Write down a list of these things and make a plan to incorporate more of them into your life.

2. ***Set meaningful goals:*** Having goals gives us direction and purpose. Think about what you want to achieve in life and set meaningful goals that align with your values and purpose. Write down your goals and create a plan to achieve them. Remember, it's okay to have small, achievable goals as well as big, long-term ones.

3. ***Cultivate gratitude:*** Gratitude has been shown to increase happiness and well-being. Make a habit of listing three things you are grateful for each day. This can be done in a journal, or you can share it with others. Focusing on what you are grateful for helps you to appreciate what you have and keeps you focused on the positive aspects of your life.

4. ***Build strong relationships:*** Investing in your relationships is an important part of living a fulfilling life. Spend time with the people you love and make an effort to build strong connections with others. Whether it's a family member, friend, or colleague, having strong relationships can bring joy, support, and a sense of belonging to your life.

5. ***Practice self-care:*** Taking care of your physical and mental health is essential for living a fulfilling life. Make sure to eat well, get enough sleep, and engage in physical activity. Take breaks and find time for activities that bring you peace and relaxation, such as yoga, meditation, or reading.

6. ***Give back:*** Helping others can bring a sense of fulfillment and purpose to your life. Find ways to volunteer, donate, or support a cause you care about. Whether it's a local charity, a community organization, or a global movement, giving back can bring a sense of satisfaction and fulfillment that is hard to match.

7. ***Celebrate your successes:*** Finally, take time to acknowledge and celebrate your achievements, no matter how big or small. Celebrating your successes can help you feel proud and motivated to continue striving towards your goals. Whether it's a promotion at work, completing a difficult project, or simply making it through a tough week, take time to recognize your accomplishments and give yourself a pat on the back.

In conclusion, living a fulfilling life is about finding joy, purpose, and meaning in each day. It's about understanding what brings you happiness and making an effort to incorporate more of it into your life. It's about setting meaningful goals and celebrating your successes. And most importantly, it's about investing in your relationships, taking care of your physical and mental health, and giving back to others. So, go forth and live a fulfilling life!

Exercise

Exercise: Living a Fulfilled Life

1. ***Reflection:*** Take some time to reflect on what brings you joy and fulfillment. Write down a list of the activities and experiences that make you feel most fulfilled.

2. ***Gratitude:*** Start a gratitude journal and write down three things you are grateful for each day. Focus on what you have in your life, rather than what you lack.

3. ***Goal setting:*** Write down your long-term and short-term goals. Make sure they align with your values and purpose in life. Create a plan to achieve your goals.

4. ***Relationships:*** Reach out to a loved one and make plans to spend quality time together. If you have a strained relationship with someone, make an effort to resolve the conflict and strengthen your bond.

5. ***Self-care:*** Plan a self-care day for yourself. This could include activities such as a bubble bath, yoga, a walk in nature, or a massage. Make sure to prioritize self-care on a regular basis.

6. ***Giving back:*** Find a cause or organization that you are passionate about and make a plan to give back. This could be volunteering, donating, or supporting a movement.

7. ***Celebration:*** Make a list of your accomplishments and successes, no matter how big or small. Take time to acknowledge and celebrate your achievements.

8. ***Reflection:*** Take some time to reflect on the changes you have made in your life. Think about how these changes have brought you closer to a fulfilled life.

9. ***Continue to grow:*** Make a plan to continue learning and growing. This could be taking a class, learning a new skill, or trying something new.

Enjoy the journey: Finally, remember to enjoy the journey. Living a fulfilled life is not about arriving at a destination, but about finding joy, purpose, and meaning in each day. So, savor the moments and make the most of your life!

Printed by Libri Plureos GmbH in Hamburg, Germany